MICKEY MOONBEAM

MIKE BROWNLOW

BLOOMSBURY
CHILDREN'S
BOOKS

For
Barbara and Mylrea

Typeset in Century Schoolbook Infant

Published by Bloomsbury Publishing, New York, London, and Berlin
Distributed to the trade by Holtzbrinck Publishers

Library of Congress Cataloging-in-Publication Data
Brownlow, Michael.
Mickey Moonbeam / Mike Brownlow.
p.   cm.
Summary: Young Mickey, who lives on a faraway moon, receives a distress call from his pen pal, Quiggle, whose space
scooter has crashed on a nearby asteroid, and they both get a big surprise when they finally meet face to face.
ISBN-10: 1-58234-704-2 • ISBN-13: 978-1-58234-704-2
[1. Space flight—Fiction. 2. Size—Fiction. 3. Pen pals—Fiction.] I. Title.
PZ7.B82412Mic 2006   [E]—dc22   2006044455

First U.S. Edition 2006
Printed in China
1 3 5 7 9 10 8 6 4 2

Cover designed by Nina Tara

Bloomsbury Publishing, Children's Books, U.S.A.
175 Fifth Avenue, New York, NY 10010

All papers used by Bloomsbury Publishing
are natural, recyclable products made from wood
grown in well-managed forests. The manufacturing
processes conform to the environmental
regulations of the country of origin.

There is a little moon far out in space,
where rockets fly among the twinkling stars.
This is where Mickey Moonbeam lives,
with all his family and friends.

Today was a special moon-day. Mickey's pen pal Quiggle was coming to visit for the first time. Quiggle lived on a planet far away, and the two friends had never met.

BIBBLE
BIBBLE
BEEEEP!

But just as Mickey was finishing his breakfast, he heard a loud noise coming from his interstellar videophone — a distress call! Someone was in trouble!

"Help!" cried a voice. "This is Quiggle. My space scooter has broken and I've crash-landed onto Asteroid B 2672. I'm stranded!"

Mickey pressed a button on the videophone.

"Quiggle," he said, "this is Mickey. Don't worry — Asteroid B 2672 is not far from Moonbeam City. I'll come and rescue you."

Quickly Mickey climbed into his space suit,
ran to his spaceship, and prepared for takeoff.
"Set speed to super-zippy-hyper-fast," he said,
twiddling some dials. "Thrusters to max!
We have one, two, three green
lights. Moonbeam AWAY!"

With a roar, Mickey rocketed up to the stars.

ZOOM!! He flew faster than a meteor, past moons and planets, suns and satellites, until he reached the asteroid.

Mickey landed his spaceship on a
large lump of rock and looked around.
But he couldn't see Quiggle anywhere.

He pulled on his helmet and jet boots
and stepped out of the cockpit.
"Where are you?" he called to Quiggle on his radio.
"I'm here on Asteroid B 2672,"
replied his friend. "Where are you?"
Mickey was puzzled.

"I'll fly to the top of this yellow hill to get a better view," he said. But still Quiggle was nowhere in sight. "I can't see you," sighed Mickey. "And I can't see you either," said Quiggle.

Just at that moment, the ground beneath Mickey's feet began to move! "Arghh!" he shouted. "It's an asteroid-quake!"

Quiggle was confused.

"I don't feel anything," he radioed back.

"But the yellow hill is shaking!" cried Mickey.

"Yellow hill?" said Quiggle. "What yellow hill?"

Mickey was thrown this way and
that, and began to fall down the
smooth side of the hill.
Down . . .
down . . .
down . . .
until —

BUMP!

He landed on a small ledge.

Nervously, he peered over the edge.
"Great galloping galaxies!" he gasped.
"Are you all right?" called Quiggle anxiously.
"Yes," said Mickey, "but guess what?

I can see a **HUGE** eye

and a **GIANT** nose

and **ENORMOUS** ears

and a **GIGANTIC** upside-down face!

And Quiggle, the gigantic face looks just like YOU!"

Quiggle was worried.
"I don't understand," he cried.
"Where are you?"
"Look on the visor of
your helmet," said
Mickey.
Quiggle looked and
saw something small
waving at him.
"Oh!" he gasped.
"It's a teeny-weeny
little spaceman!
But Mickey, the
little spaceman
looks just like you."
"It *is* me!"
said Mickey.

And then they both understood.
The big yellow hill was
Quiggle's helmet!
"I didn't know when we
spoke on the videophone
that you were so small,"
he said.

It's not me who's so small. It's you who's so big!" laughed Mickey. "If you think I'm big," said Quiggle, "you should see my parents. Where I come from, I'm tiny!"

But their smiles turned to frowns when they looked at Quiggle's space scooter. Only one of his engines was working. The other was too broken to fix.

"And I can't give you a ride home in my spaceship," groaned Mickey, "because you're too big to fit."

Quiggle's bottom lip began to quiver.

"But if we can't fix my engine and I can't fit in your spaceship," he said, sniffing, "I might be trapped on this asteroid forever. I'll never see my mom and dad again."

Mickey thought long and hard. Suddenly he said,
"I have an idea!" And he began to crawl into the
cramped, narrow spaces in the middle
of the broken engine.

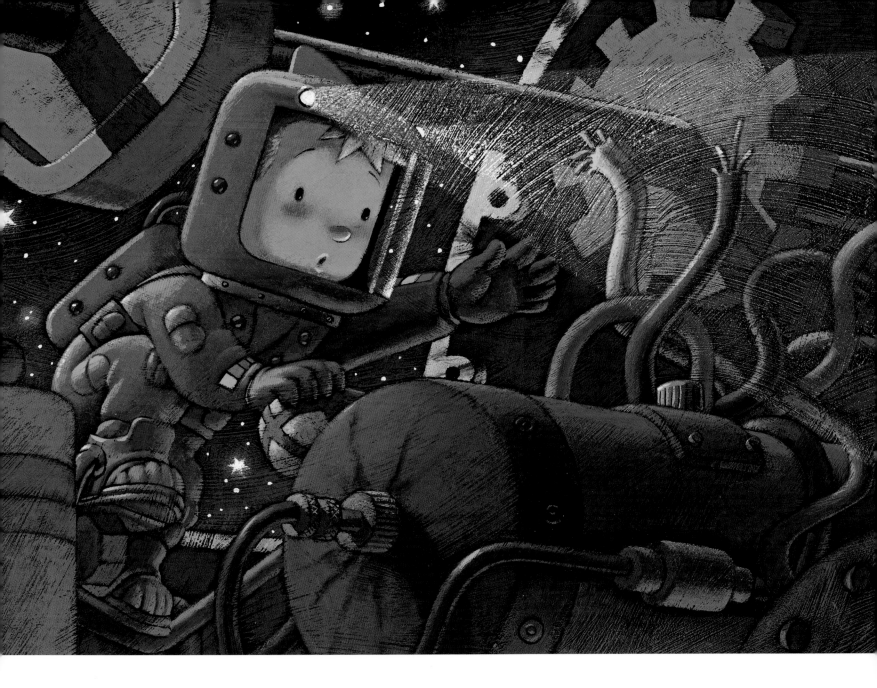

"Be careful," said Quiggle nervously. "It looks dangerous in there."

"Not far now," Mickey called back. "I can just about squeeze through. It's lucky I'm so small!"

A couple of moon-minutes later, Mickey
reappeared carrying a bundle of wires.
"Now, can you move my spaceship over here to your scooter?"
"Of course!" said Quiggle, and he picked up
Mickey's ship as easily as if it were a feather.
"It's lucky I'm so big and strong! What's your plan?"

"Let's use my spaceship instead
of your broken engine,"
answered Mickey. "We can tie it
to your scooter with this wire."
So that's what they did.

"Good work!" they agreed when they'd finished.
"Now let's prepare for takeoff!"
"Thrusters to max!" shouted Quiggle.
"We have one, two, three green lights!"
cried Mickey.
"Quiggle and Moonbeam AWAY!"
It worked! The two blasted off the asteroid and rocketed all
the way back to Moonbeam City.

While the space scooter was being repaired, Mickey showed
Quiggle the house where he lived with his family.
"The next time you come to visit us," smiled Mickey, "we'll
have to make the door bigger!"